OTTO
THE
OWL
WHO
LOVED
POETRY

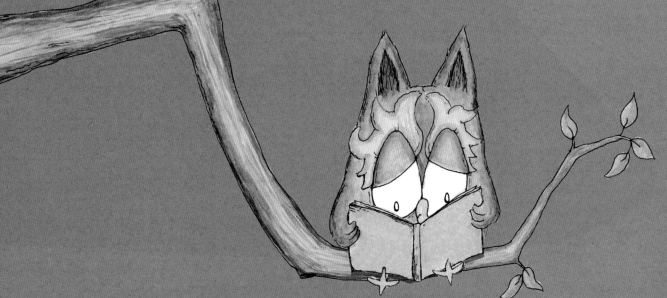

Vern Kousky

Nancy Paulsen Books ✺ An Imprint of Penguin Group (USA)

Nancy Paulsen Books
Published by the Penguin Group
Penguin Group (USA) LLC
375 Hudson Street
New York, NY 10014

USA | Canada | UK | Ireland | Australia
New Zealand | India | South Africa | China
penguin.com
A Penguin Random House Company

Library of Congress Cataloging-in-Publication Data
Kousky, Vern, author, illustrator.
Otto the owl who loved poetry / Vern Kousky.
pages cm
Summary: "Otto the Owl doesn't fit in because he would rather recite poetry than hunt mice"—Provided by publisher.
[1. Poetry—Fiction. 2. Individuality—Fiction. 3. Owls—Fiction. 4. Mice—Fiction.] I. Title.
PZ7.K8558Ott 2015 [E]—dc23 2014012282

Manufactured in China by South China Printing Co. Ltd.
ISBN 978-0-399-16440-8
3 5 7 9 10 8 6 4 2

Design by Marikka Tamura. Text set in Paradigm.
The illustrations are mixed media assembled on a computer.

for Anna

Otto is not like the other owls of the forest.

You see, owls are supposed to roost in the hollow of a tree.

But Otto would rather read books.

And owls are supposed to hunt
in the dark of night.

But Otto would rather make friends.

Owls, of course, aren't really supposed to recite poetry. But when the other owls are roosting or hunting, Otto finds a secret spot and recites his favorite poems.

Let us go then, you and I,
When the evening is spread out
against the sky . . .

One snowy night,
Otto's secret is discovered.

*The cold wind burns my face, and blows
Its frosty pepper up my nose. . . .*

Now, when the other owls
see Otto, they laugh and shout,
"Look! It's Blotto!"

"Here comes Blotto the Bard!"

On his nightly walks, Otto sighs and sadly wonders, "Why do all the owls tease me? What could possibly be wrong with poetry?"

At last, he decides to run away.

As Otto wanders through the forest,
the moonlight guides him.
"Well, dear Moon," he says,
"I guess it's just you and me now."

And suddenly, he has an idea for a poem,
the very first of his own creation!

Dear Moon, you must be lonely
so high up in the sky.
I'm sure your heart's so heavy,
sometimes you want to cry.

But dear Moon, please do not worry.
I've a message here to send:
I'm with you every evening.
Dear Moon, you're my best friend!

Otto is surprised
to see dozens of
tiny faces looking
up at him.

He is even more surprised
to hear dozens of tiny voices
begin to shout, "More! More!"

So Otto delights the mice with another poem.

I think that I shall never see
A poem lovely as a tree. . . .
A tree that may in summer wear
A nest of robins in her hair . . .

Otto now knows that poetry should
be shared with more than just the moon
and the stars.
Poetry should be shared with everyone.

And so, when a few owls find Otto in the forest one spring night, he does not run and hide. Instead, he proudly recites:

I'm nobody! Whooo are you?
Are you nobody, too? . . .

The more the owls listen, the less
they feel like laughing.
    And when the poem is finished,
they all hoot and holler, "More! More!
Whoo! Whoo! Whoo!!"

The next night, another owl
recites a new favorite poem.

Whooo has seen the wind?
Neither I nor you:
But when the leaves hang trembling
The wind is passing through. . . .

And even a little mouse
is inspired to write a poem
of her own.

Oh, my beautiful hunk of cheese,
you smell so sweet and good!
Oh, my beautiful hunk of cheese,
I'd marry you if I could!

And so now, thanks to Otto,
every night the forest comes alive
with the glorious sounds of poetry.

Here are Otto's favorite famous poems:

Let us go then, you and I,
When the evening is spread out against the sky . . .
   —from "The Love Song of J. Alfred Prufrock" by T. S. Eliot

The cold wind burns my face, and blows
Its frosty pepper up my nose. . . .
       —from "Winter-Time" by Robert Louis Stevenson

I think that I shall never see
A poem lovely as a tree. . . .
A tree that may in summer wear
A nest of robins in her hair . . .
         —from "Trees" by Joyce Kilmer

I'm nobody! Who are you?
Are you nobody, too? . . .
   —from "I'm nobody! Who are you?" by Emily Dickinson

Who has seen the wind?
Neither I nor you:
But when the leaves hang trembling
The wind is passing through. . . .
   —from "Who Has Seen the Wind?" by Christina Rossetti

All other poems by Vern Kousky.